A Pony Named Patches

CHARMING PONIES

A Pony Named Patches

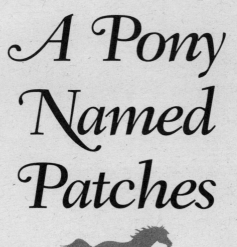

LOIS SZYMANSKI

HarperFestival®
A Division of HarperCollins*Publishers*

This book is dedicated to my writers support group:
Shelley Sykes, Melissa Wyatt, Laura Wiess, Livy
Sykes, Debbie McConnell, and Terri Coppersmith.
More than just birds of a feather, they are true family.

A Pony Named Patches

one

As the land rumbled by outside, Matt settled down in his seat and leaned his head against the cool window. Even though it was only the middle of May, already the heat outside gave everything a hazy glaze. He was grateful for the air conditioning inside the car.

It wouldn't be long until they arrived at Chincoteague Island and Matt was anxious. He couldn't wait to see the wild ponies on Assateague again. He had spent a week there last year . . . just he and his dad. Back then, they had read *Misty of Chincoteague* and *Stormy, Misty's Foal* out loud to each other in the evenings.

But this time would be different. This time there would be no Dad. This was the beginning of life without him.

The car passed over the arching bridge onto Chincoteague Island, wandered down Main Street, then turned into a driveway. Matt recognized Aunt Marleen and Uncle Bob's battered white pickup truck in front of their house. Matt remembered the pickup pulling up in front of his row house in Baltimore. Aunt Marleen and Uncle Bob took him fishing, hiking, and camping. They taught him to love the country. That was before they had moved to Chincoteague.

The front door slammed as Uncle Bob and Aunt Marleen came running out. "We thought you'd never arrive," Aunt Marleen exclaimed.

"I forgot how far it was from Baltimore to here," Mom said with a smile. Matt was happy to see her smile. She hadn't done much of that lately.

Before he knew it Aunt Marleen folded him in her arms in a big bear hug and he relaxed. Maybe it wouldn't be so bad, being sent to spend the summer with them.

Matt pedaled his bike furiously, up and over the arching bridge that led from Chincoteague Island to Assateague Island. He'd decided to come alone this first time. He stopped at the top and brushed his hair back from his eyes. Below him the waters of the channel spread out with life. There were black ducks and wood ducks floating lazily on the choppy water. A snowy egret picked its way through the tall cattails. Matt lifted his camera, pushed his glasses up on his nose, and snapped a picture of the egret.

Shading his eyes against the glare of water and sun, he watched a man and a woman crabbing. The man tugged gently on a hand line as the woman stood with her net poised, waiting to scoop a crab from the bait at the end of the line. Their bushel basket was nearly half full of crabs already.

Suddenly, watching them was too hard and Matt turned away. He remembered his father and himself standing in that same spot on that same shoreline.

Matt pushed off on his bicycle, letting the speed build as he drifted down from the top of the bridge. Faster and faster he went, almost blinded by his tears. Tree limbs reached out from the edge of the blacktop bike trail, slapping his arms and face as he darted from side to side on the path. Matt braked his bicycle and rolled to a stop. He stood on the edge of the trail, sheltered by the overgrown myrtle bushes. He let the tears stream down his face. It was so unfair! Other kids had their fathers. Why did his dad have to die?

Matt heard voices coming toward him. They floated closer on the breeze. He wiped away his tears. He didn't want anyone to see him crying.

Matt pedaled past two women and on down the

trail past the ranger station. The wind rustled in the leaves overhead as he passed through an archway of trees and out into the sun. Matt pushed on past the low-lying marsh areas, stopping only to take pictures of the Sika deer in the distance. The tall grass tickled his legs when he pedaled close to the edge of the trail. Queen Anne's lace, black-eyed Susans, and daisies swayed among the grass with many other wildflowers. It was so peaceful here. He was glad he had decided to come.

Matt turned onto a path marked PONY TRAIL and entered the cooler forest. The only sound was the rustling of trees and a few calls from sea gulls. The smell of pine and myrtle filled the air and mingled with the salty ocean scent.

A small grove of loblolly pines came into view. It was a perfect hideaway. Matt propped his bike against a tree and reached for his knapsack. He sat crosslegged on a bed of pine needles and turned over the sack. His picnic lunch of a sandwich and an apple awaited him.

As he crunched the apple, Matt peered through the greenery. He could just make out the waters of the bay in the distance. Something moved in the trees. Matt hoped it was a pony, but when he looked closer he found it was just a fox squirrel scampering to another tree. If only he could find the ponies and get some pictures for his collection.

Suddenly a noise punctured his thoughts. He stopped chewing and listened. There it was! A low moan followed by a grunting sound. Even though it wasn't very loud, it sounded as if it were near! Matt jumped to his feet and strained his ears. It seemed to be coming from the bushes.

Dropping his apple core, he took a step into the undergrowth. Cautiously, he parted the limbs of a large bush and peered through.

There was the source of the sound, a yellow and white pinto mare lying on her side. She was scrubby in appearance, with a stomach that bulged upward with each heaving breath that she took. Her white markings were splattered with mud and her mane and tail were matted with burrs. She lifted her head and rolled her eyes back at Matt, but made no attempt to stand.

"That's strange," Matt mumbled. He wondered if she was sick. The mare groaned again. Her stomach tightened and swelled before his eyes and she reached back toward her tail, nipping at the air as if she were in pain.

Then Matt realized why the mare did not get up. "She's having a baby!" he gasped.

The mare jumped at the sound of his voice. Then she seemed to forget him and focus only on the birth.

Two tiny front hooves emerged, wrapped in a veil of white. The yellow pinto pushed and strained. Sweat rose across her shoulders and her mane clung to her neck limply. Matt watched in silence, not wanting to disturb her again.

With a strong push the head came out, followed by the neck and shoulders. Then the rest of the foal slid out in a rush.

Matt took off his glasses and wiped them with the

back of his shirt, shaking from the wonder of it all! He wanted to shout to the top of the trees. He wanted to tell someone that he had seen a miracle! But the person he wanted to tell had left early that morning, heading back to Baltimore alone. If he couldn't tell his mom, Matt decided it would be his own secret.

The yellow pinto scrambled to her feet, breaking the shroud that covered her foal. She snorted and rolled her eyes at Matt again. It seemed she decided Matt was not dangerous. She turned her tail to him and sniffed the newborn. Then she began methodically licking.

Matt bent down to get a better look. He thought the foal was in a strange position. The front legs were folded underneath and its belly was twisted upward. It looked strange, but the little fellow seemed to be just fine.

The newborn looked bright and shiny and clean compared to his mother. Matt peered at the underbelly of the foal and saw that it was a boy. He was white with dark brown patches crisscrossing his body in uneven shapes. He looked so tiny and fragile and weak!

The pinto nuzzled her son softly, pushing him to stand. He scrambled up on two shaky front legs, weaving back and forth unsteadily. Then the colt fell. Matt held his breath. He wanted to rush forward and help the colt to stand, but Matt knew better than to interfere.

The colt was not a quitter. He pushed forward again, lurching upward on two splayed front legs. This time his back legs followed and he stood swaying. He noisily rooted for his mother's milk, then found it and began to suckle.

Matt smiled. He remembered his camera. Matt fumbled with the strap, uncapped the lens, and began to shoot frame after frame. The mother pony ignored him completely. She returned to the job of cleaning her patchy little colt as he drank greedily.

The waters of the bay were gently lapping the shelly beach sand below them and the sun was sinking into the top of the trees. Matt hadn't thought about the time for so long. Now he lifted his arm to check his watch. It was seven-thirty. Time to get home to Aunt Marleen and Uncle Bob for dinner.

The pony nudged her new son forward gently. Matt knew that she would be going back to her herd. He knew that the ponies gathered in herds for protection. A single stallion watched over and guarded each band of mares and foals. Matt wished he could live like a wild pony, protected and sheltered in a herd, instead of being pushed onto a relative for the summer.

Turning toward the mare and the foal, he took one last picture as they pushed aside the undergrowth and disappeared. It was getting late and he knew he should be getting along too.

"But I'll be back," Matt told the whispering trees. "I'll be back to see that patchy colt again."

two

Matt coasted down the empty driveway, bumping and slowing as he hit the gravel part. Just short of the house, he stopped. There was a boy sitting on the front step. He pushed his legs out in front of himself, yawned, and stretched.

Matt studied the kid from beneath the shadow of a pine tree at the driveway's edge. He was tall and thin, with a shock of untamed hair and just a smattering of freckles. He looked comfortable, as if he had been there before.

The front door opened and Uncle Bob stepped out. He pushed back his sandy hair and said something to the kid. They both laughed together and Matt felt a little jealous. Then he realized it was silly to be jealous.

But he felt like he didn't belong. He wondered what his mom was doing at home.

The door opened again and Aunt Marleen stepped onto the porch. She looked down the driveway anxiously. Then she spotted Matt.

"There you are!" she called. Matt pedaled slowly toward them. "We were beginning to worry about you, kiddo!"

"I lost track of time," he answered quietly.

"I do that all the time," said Uncle Bob. "Especially when I'm over on Assateague. Something about that place makes you forget everything else."

"Yes," Matt answered, feeling the magic of the

birth all over again.

"This is Danny," Aunt Marleen said. Her hand settled on the boy's shoulder and he grinned at her. "Danny lives just up the road. He helps us out a lot with the leaves in fall and the snow in winter. I asked him to have dinner with us tonight. I thought it would be nice if you two met."

"Hi," Matt mumbled awkwardly. He was startled when Danny slapped him on the back good-naturedly.

"It's good to finally meet you!" he said.

"Finally?"

"Yeah! Your aunt talks about you all the time. Ever since I've known her she's been telling me all about her nephew, Matt. She says you used to go camping with them and stuff."

Matt relaxed and a smile played at the corners of his mouth. They had talked about him! That felt good.

"When Miss Marleen told me you were coming for the summer I started making plans. She said you were nine years old, just like me. It'll be cool having someone my own age around."

"What about Sherry, next door?" Uncle Bob teased.

"Come on, Mr. Bob! Cut it out! Sherry's a girl!"

"Well I'm a girl, too," Aunt Marleen teased. "And I happen to be the girl who cooked dinner tonight, so you guys better behave and get in here before it's too cold to eat."

Over dinner Danny told Matt some of the things he had planned. "I need a business partner. How would you like to go into business together?"

Matt swallowed a bite of chicken. "What kind of business?"

"The bait business. I've been reading a book on raising fishing worms. The book says they like to live in rabbit manure!"

Matt swallowed again and the food almost caught on the giggle rising in his throat. "Rabbit manure?" he croaked.

"Yeah! Rabbit manure!"

Danny looked so serious that Matt couldn't help it. He laughed right out loud. "Where are we going to get rabbit manure?"

"No problem. My little sister has four pet rab-bits. I already checked it out and the book is right. The worms are practically having a party under the pens! All we gotta do is dig them up and sell them!"

"Believe me, Matt," Uncle Bob said, "Danny is not kidding!" He winked across the table.

"Okay," Matt said, with his face as straight as he could hold it. "I'll be your worming partner!"

He reached over and grasped Danny's out-stretched hand and as they shook on it, Matt realized that he was going to like this partnership.

"You cut that one right in half, you dingbat!"

"Well, how was I supposed to know it was there? Look at the bright side. Now we have two!"

Matt grinned. "Maybe next time we should knock before we dig!"

"Well, we got the bottom of the bucket covered. That's not bad. We've only been out here about twenty minutes."

"Count 'em. See how many we have."

As Danny held up the squiggling worms one at a time and counted out loud, Matt thought about fall, when he would be going home. He thought about the sweltering heat of blacktop and concrete streets and he did not want to go home. Then he thought about his mother there all alone, and he felt sad. He sunk his trowel deep into the soft manure and dirt again and directed his thoughts back to the worm business.

"We have six dozen," Danny said. "I've been checking around. Worms this size go for about two dollars a dozen."

Matt looked into the bucket. They weren't regular worms. They were night crawlers and they were huge! You couldn't find worms this size in the city.

"Two dollars a dozen," Matt mused. "That seems like a lot, but if we sell them for two dollars a dozen we'll have to spend a lot of time trying to find customers. Why don't we sell them for less, say a dollar or a dollar-fifty a dozen and take them to the bait shops on the island. I bet we could sell a lot more that way and we wouldn't have to spend our whole summer sitting around trying to sell them."

Matt was thinking about the colt. He wanted to save time to ride to Assateague to see him. He needed to see the colt. He needed to get more photos. There was something else that made the colt special and important to him. But he couldn't figure out exactly what it was.

Matt said none of this out loud. He wasn't ready to share the colt yet. He wondered if Danny could understand how important the little foal was, anyway.

"That sounds pretty good," Danny finally answered. His voice jerked Matt back to the worming at hand. "But on the days we have extra worms we can sell them on the road for the extra buck too!"

Matt grunted. "If we're going to sell that many worms we better get busy!"

three

The shrill jingle of a telephone rang out, waking Matt. He pushed back the blankets, threw his legs over the side of the bed, and sat up. Cobwebs of sleep filled his mind and he shook his head to clear them.

The phone stopped ringing. Matt heard Aunt Marleen talking on the downstairs extension.

"Yes. Yes, he's fine," she was saying. Then there

was a pause. "He's asleep right now. Do you want me to wake him?" Then there was another pause.

Matt grabbed his robe from the chair and hurried downstairs.

"He's been having a wonderful time. We introduced him to a boy we knew and they hit it off great." Pause. "Yes. How about you? How are you doing?" Pause. "Okay. Well, I'll tell him that you called."

Matt leaped down the last two steps. "Don't hang up!" he shouted. "I'm awake."

"Hold on, Margaret. Are you still there? Matt's here now. He must have heard the phone."

He took the phone from Aunt Marleen's hand.

"Hi, Mom!"

"Hi, Matt." She sounded so quiet. "How do you like it down there?"

"Great, Mom. I mean I really like it. Last week I rode my bike over to Assateague and I saw some wild ponies."

"That's terrific. I heard you made a friend, too?"

"Yeah. Danny. He's kind of crazy, but he's nice.

He makes me laugh a lot."

"I guess I can stop worrying about you then."

"Are you okay, Mom?"

There was a moment of silence, then a sigh.

"I'm okay, Matt. I just miss you. It's real quiet without you."

Matt felt tears welling up behind his eyes. He could picture her sitting alone at the dining-room table and it made him sad.

"Can't you come down?" he asked. "Why can't you just get a job down here? If you did, Aunt Mars would be with me during the day and you wouldn't have to worry. I miss you, too."

"You know, that might not be a bad idea. I'll think about it, kiddo!" Suddenly her voice was cheerier. Matt didn't know if it was his idea or if she was putting on a happy act to make him feel better.

"Listen. I gotta go now and you have to go back to bed. Sorry I woke you."

"Bye, Mom. See you soon?"

"Before you know it. I love you."

"Me, too. Bye."

There was a click on the other end of the line. Matt stood there for a moment, cradling the dead receiver against his ear. He hung it up then and climbed the stairs to his room.

He felt drained. He missed his dad and now he missed his mom even more.

Matt squatted down in the tall weeds and watched the herd. The stallion paced nervously around his band of mares.

"How does he know I'm here?" Matt muttered out loud.

The stallion's head jerked up and he snorted toward the bushes where Matt hid. Matt lowered himself deeper into the greenery and forced himself to stay quiet until the stallion had resumed his grazing.

Matt let out his breath. He scanned the herd.

"There she is!" he breathed.

The yellow and white pinto was grazing, away from the other ponies. The colt was nursing at her side.

All at once she moved forward a few steps, jerking the colt's dinner away, and he stamped his hoof with a comical, startled look.

Matt giggled out loud. The stallion's head flew up and he peered at the bushes again.

The yellow pinto gave her son a shove as another mare wandered too close to them. They trotted away from the herd toward Matt.

Matt held his breath as they approached. He was amazed at how quickly the colt's legs had become steady.

Mare and colt had almost reached him when a rabbit leaped from the bushes at their feet. The mare only glanced at it, but the colt shied sideways, then stopped to stare at it curiously.

The mare whinnied. It looked to Matt like she was telling the colt, "A rabbit is nothing to stop for! Come along!"

Matt grabbed his camera and stood slowly.

The mare stopped short and the colt almost ran smack into her tail. The colt peered from behind his mother to see what the interruption was. As he stared out from behind the shelter of her sweeping tail, Matt focused the camera and snapped a picture.

The colt jumped, then stepped closer.

Matt snapped another picture, then another. The colt stood transfixed as the camera clicked.

"Hello, little fella!" Matt whispered. He stretched his palm out toward the toylike colt that was less than thirty feet away. "Come closer, little patches."

All at once the yellow mare shot forward. Matt ducked and jumped back. He was afraid. Was the mare going to charge him?

Matt tripped over a tree stump, then turned back in awe. Instead of charging at Matt, the mare nipped her son sharply, chasing him into the herd. Feeling her urgency, the whole herd whirled away. The yellow pinto and her patchy colt fell into step with the rest of the herd.

"Patches!" Matt said out loud. "It's a perfect name."

Then he thought about the danger he had put

himself in. He was excited now. He had never been this close to a wild pony, or anything wild for that matter! He gripped the camera tightly. Inside were the greatest close-up shots he had ever taken!

"You'll get used to me," Matt whispered. "I'll be back," he told them, "and you're gonna trust me before the summer is over."

four

Danny slid the wire handle of the bucket over his bike's handlebars.

"We can carry them like this," he said. He was talking about the buckets of dirt and squiggling earthworms they had collected over the past week.

Matt slid a bucket onto one side of the bike's handlebars, then another one on the other side.

"I guess it will work . . . if we're careful." He pointed a sneakered toe at one last bucket, which sat in the gravel driveway between them. "You get that one."

Danny leaned down and lifted the last bucket onto his handlebars, opposite the first one. "These empty paint cans your Uncle Bob found are perfect for carrying worms!"

Matt nodded, then pushed off, his bike swaying from side to side with the rhythm of buckets swinging on the handlebars. Once he gained some speed, the swaying lessened and he felt more in control of the bike. He glanced over his shoulder at Danny.

Danny had not gained control of his bike. He was wobbling even worse than Matt had. The weight of the worm buckets pulled Danny's handlebars back and forth and he zigzagged down the driveway. Matt turned forward again and concentrated on keeping his own bike in line.

Even though it was still early in the day, it was already terribly hot and sticky. Droplets of sweat rolled down Danny's face. He puffed as he pedaled, trying to force his bike into taking a straight path down the driveway.

"I don't think this is going to work," he puffed. The words were barely out of his mouth when the handlebars jerked rapidly to the right, jackknifing his bicycle in the middle of the driveway. He tried to catch himself with his right leg, but it was too late. The side of his bike caught him and threw him to the ground. The bucket on the right side hit the road with a resounding *thud*. The force of it sprayed dirt and worms out of the top of the bucket.

Matt hit his brakes when he heard the crash.

"You all right?" he called over his shoulder as he slid his worm buckets to the ground.

"Criminy!" Danny shouted.

Matt turned to check on his friend. He was ready to help him to his feet, but when he saw Danny, all he could do was laugh.

Danny sat in the gravel with the bike pinning his legs. The bucket of worms sat neatly beside him, looking as if it had been placed there with great care. But it had really landed with so much force that Danny's hair and face were covered with dirt, and a worm hung precariously from his right ear!

Danny spit dirt out of his mouth and glared at Matt.

"Very funny!" he said, as he picked a worm out of his hair. "Very funny!"

"I'm sorry," Matt said, "but you do look ridiculous!"

Danny grinned as he pushed the bike off himself. "Yeah, I guess I do. I guess we could call this the revenge of the worms!"

He brushed off his pants and stood, shaking the dirt from his hair.

"You okay?"

"I'm fine, but look at all the worms I ruined."

Matt looked at the worms writhing in the gravel dust. One bucket was on its side. A small amount of dirt had spilled out the top, but no worms had been lost. It was the innocent-looking can, sitting upright, that had sprayed out its contents.

"Yup. Those worms are goners for sure."

"It's only about half the bucket," Danny said, peering into the mess.

"Don't worry about it. There's plenty more where they came from," Matt reassured him. "Let's just get these to the bait shop before they bite the dust, too! Think you can handle a bucket and a half?"

Danny grinned broadly. "No problem," he said, mounting his bike.

Matt and Danny wove their way down the driveway and onto the hot paved road. It was only a half-mile to Pringle's Bait Shop. They had talked to Mr. Pringle only a day ago and he had promised them one dollar a dozen for all the worms they could get.

Matt patted his empty pocket and thought about what he could do with his share of the money they made. They had worked hard digging under the rabbit pens. At night they had gone outside with flashlights and searched in the moist grass for the nightcrawlers and they had found plenty. Before

Danny had spilled the bucket they'd had twenty-six dozen worms. That would have been twenty-six dollars to split between them! Even with the worms they'd lost, it would still be over twenty dollars.

"What are you going to do with your half of the money?" Matt called.

"I don't know. How 'bout you?"

"I'm not sure yet," Matt answered, but already he had an idea. Maybe he could buy his mom a gift and send it to her. Whatever it was, it had to be good though. It had to be something to cheer her up— something special. But he didn't know what.

Mr. Pringle didn't count the worms in the spilled bucket. When they told him what had happened he laughed out loud and slapped Danny on the back.

"Before we spilled them we had twenty-six dozen," Matt explained. "Now we aren't sure exactly how many we have."

Mr. Pringle pulled a wad of money from his back pocket and counted out twenty-six dollars.

"I'd say you earned it," he said, still grinning

from the idea of Danny with worms in his hair. "When do you think you'll have more? This is my busy season, you know?"

Matt was all ready to say a week, when Danny piped up.

"Give us a few days."

As they pedaled away from the bait shop, Matt shot Danny a look. "Are you crazy?" he asked. "It took us a week to get those!"

"We'll work harder then. Think of all that *money!*" He drew out the word money as if he were savoring it.

Matt shook his head. "You're too much," he said, trying to hide the hint of anger he felt. This worm business was cutting into his time with the colt.

Matt veered off to the left at the intersection. "I'll catch you later," he told Danny. "I gotta pick up some film I dropped off a few days ago."

"Okay. See you tomorrow!" Danny answered as they split. Matt headed for the pharmacy, where he'd left the film to be developed. A swarm of mosquitoes followed him and he pedaled faster, trying to lose them. He knew it was hopeless, of course. It was nearing the end of June, and on Chincoteague that spelled mosquitoes! Lots of them!

Shutting the door to his room, Matt sat down on the bed and opened the packet of pictures. One by one he pulled them from the paper envelope.

There was the first shot. A dim view of the back of Aunt Marleen and Uncle Bob's house, taken from the stand of pines, on the first evening of his arrival. There hadn't been enough light and the shot was blurry and dark.

Next were some pictures of egrets and Sika deer, then the incredible shots he'd taken just after Patches was born. The colt was wet and wobbly and the pictures were perfect. But the best pictures in the bunch were the close-ups of Patches peering into the camera from the bushes. The colt's face was mostly brown, with a thin white snip running down the nose. In one picture, the mare's nose touched Patches's flank.

Matt hadn't noticed it at the time, but now he saw a look of curiosity on the mare's face, too! Maybe he could get her to like him, too!

Matt spread the pictures out on the bed. It had cost six dollars to develop them. He still had seven dollars of the worm money left.

Matt picked the four best shots to have enlarged. He would hang three of them over his bed, two of the wet colt just after birth, and one of the colt peering into the camera.

The fourth picture he would enlarge was a close-up and the best one of all. In it, the colt looked fuzzy and whiskery and comical. His eyelashes were thick and dark. His eyes were dreamy and liquid brown. It was for his mom. She would love it. It was the perfect present.

five

Matt pulled the blankets up around his chin and shivered. A cool breeze blew through the open bedroom window. Thunder rumbled and lightning flashed as a summer storm moved over the island. Each flash lit the room then left it again in shadowy darkness. At home he would have crept down to the living room to be with his family. They would have sat together with lanterns and candles close by, just in case the power went out. Dad would have told stories about the old days when people had to use lanterns and candles for light every evening, and not just for storms when the power went out. It always seemed cozy and safe when they were together like that. Now, as Matt huddled under the sheets, he realized how much he missed home. He got up and wandered down the stairs.

In the kitchen, Aunt Marleen was pouring herself a glass of milk. When she saw Matt, she poured a glass for him, too. He pulled his chair up to the table and sipped his milk.

"Matt? Are you all right?" Aunt Marleen stood behind his chair and put an arm over his shoulder. "Did you have a bad dream?"

"No." Matt didn't want to talk about his feelings. He forced a smile. "I was just thinking about the ponies I saw on Assateague. What do they do when it rains?"

"They find a place to keep dry under the thick pine trees."

"What if it rains too hard?"

Aunt Marleen saw the worry lines on Matt's face. "The water doesn't hurt them," she answered. "Why? Is there a special one you're thinking about?"

All at once Matt wanted to tell his Aunt Marleen about his secret colt. "Yeah! Remember the first day I biked over to Assateague Island?"

Aunt Marleen nodded.

"I saw a colt being born that day. It was so neat. Since then I've been following him all over the island. Last time I almost touched him!"

A smile spread over Aunt Marleen's face. "Maybe I can go with you to see him sometime?" she asked.

Matt leaped up. "You can see him now! The pictures I took . . . I'll show you!"

He raced up the steps to get the photos. It felt good to share the secret. Aunt Marleen was as crazy about the ponies as he was. Maybe tomorrow he would take her to see Patches! She would love the colt, too!

* * *

Aunt Marleen had too many errands to run the next day, so Matt went to the island alone. It was July the second already, and for the first time Matt thought about Pony Penning Day. On the last Wednesday of every July the firemen of Chincoteague Island would round up the ponies and herd them into a channel of the bay. The ponies would have to swim to Chincoteague, where they were paraded down Main Street and penned on the carnival grounds. It was an annual event and the talk of the town. People came from miles away to see the ponies swim.

The day after the swim, most of the foals would be separated from their mothers and auctioned off! He might lose Patches! Each year some of the ponies escaped or hid so well that the firemen missed them. Matt hoped that Patches would not be forced to swim the channel. He hoped the yellow-spotted mare would hide her son well. He didn't want Patches to be separated from his momma and sold to a stranger!

Matt thought about all of this as he searched for

the herd. He checked the meadow where he'd seen them last and the stand of pine trees where they often rested. No ponies.

He slapped at a mosquito, then pulled a can of bug spray from his knapsack and sprayed a huge mist around and over his head. Next he coated his arms and legs with the spray.

"How can they stand the mosquitoes?" He muttered out loud. "The ponies don't have bug spray to protect them!"

Finally, Matt found the herd. They stood on the beach with their backs to the ocean. The cool salty breeze that came off the water ruffled their manes and tails. Matt moved closer as he watched.

Patches was watching his momma swipe away the insects with her nonstop tail. Then he tried to do the same. But his little wisp of a broom tail did nothing but stir up the dust in his furry coat! Once he switched it so hard that it went round and round like a helicopter, but the flies and mosquitoes settled right back down. Matt laughed out loud. Patches jerked his head up and eyed Matt.

Matt moved closer. The stallion eyed him warily, but he seemed to have grown accustomed to Matt and his clicking black box. Matt raised his camera and took a picture of the brown stallion. The stallion held his head high. He flared his nostrils wide as he stood over the herd with a look of pride.

Patches had wised up. He sidled up to his momma and let her long ropy tail swipe the insects away from his face and body. Matt eased himself closer and closer, stopping to dump sand from his sneakers. As he moved forward, his toes caressing the warm sand, the stallion moved forward, too. Nudging the yellow-spotted mare first, the stallion led the whole herd right into the ocean surf! They turned and stood facing the beach, with the waves breaking over their backs.

Matt smiled as Patches and the mare ran in the surf, splashing up the cooling ocean mists. Then, up the beach they came, sliding to a stop not far from him.

Patches licked his lips and stood still. The wind

ruffled his fuzzy mane. He watched Matt watching him. The colt seemed used to Matt now. After all, he had seen Matt many times since his birth.

They stood like that for a long while, until a brave sea gull landed on Patches's back. Then the colt was off again, leaving tiny hoofprints in the wet sand. Matt snapped another picture.

Patches stopped to eye a little brown sandpiper curiously. Then he stepped closer to Matt. Matt stretched his hand out and touched the velvety muzzle. It was so soft! Gently Matt stroked Patches's nose.

This time it was Matt who drew away. He didn't want to push the mare. She had cautiously allowed the touch. Matt felt certain that she would allow more if he went slowly.

Matt's watch told him it was getting late. He knew Aunt Marleen would soon have dinner ready. So he turned his back on the herd and trudged up the beach to where he'd left his bike. The colt trailed behind him for awhile, until the mare whinnied shrilly, calling him back to her on the double.

As he pedaled down the road toward home, Matt ached inside. Not only did he miss his dad, but his mother too. On top of that, he couldn't shake the foreboding feeling that filled him when he thought about Pony Penning.

He knew the colt was his, inside where it really counted, and nothing could take that away. Nothing, that is, except Pony Penning.

six

"Lunch, guys!" Aunt Marleen's voice rang out. Danny and Matt each looked up.

"Man, am I glad it's lunch time," Danny said. "My back is killing me." He stood up, slowly unbending his back as he rose from his knees.

Matt stuck his trowel in the ground, brushed the dirt from his hands, and stood, too, "This is no good," he said. "We gotta go back to looking under the rabbit pens or picking them up at night with a flashlight."

Danny glanced at the bottom of the worm can, where less than a dozen worms wriggled, most of them disappointingly small. He threw a handful of dirt over them and nodded.

"I thought the garden would be a great spot for worms. In the spring when we plant I always see plenty."

"Maybe we should try your garden next time," Matt suggested.

"There's got to be an easier way than this. We're supposed to have another ten dozen worms for Mr. Pringle by Friday!"

"I ought to say I told you so!" Matt mumbled.

"You just did," Danny shot back. "We'll just have to go see Mr. Pringle and tell him that we can't get as many worms as we thought we could."

"You mean as many as *you* thought we could!"

"Okay! Okay! I give. The only thing I could see was all that money! But don't give up yet. We might make it. Remember the last two orders? You said we wouldn't make them on time either. But we did!"

"Yeah," Matt mumbled as he remembered the rush to fill those orders. It really hadn't been all that bad and he did have fifty dollars saved because of all their work . . . even after he paid to develop his film!

"All we gotta do is spend more nights picking up night crawlers with a flashlight."

"All right," Matt answered. An idea was growing in his mind. Maybe if they worked as hard as Danny wanted, he could earn enough money to buy Patches at Pony Penning!

The boys washed their muddy hands under the spigot and headed for the picnic table, where Aunt Marleen had left their lunch. They were both quiet for awhile as they munched on chips and tuna fish sandwiches.

Matt was watching the birds that fluttered in the pine trees around them. He eyed a mother sparrow as she plucked worms from the earth and carried them in her beak to the nest she had in a corner rafter of the shed. Two babies stretched from the nest, peeping. They were covered with bluish-white fuzz and their beaks seemed almost as big as they were!

Danny was watching the sparrow too, and it gave him an idea.

"There *is* an easier way to get worms!" he told Matt excitedly.

"Oh, yeah. Well, let's hear it then!"

Matt was prepared for some crazy idea. Danny always had some cockamamie scheme cooking. He watched the sparrow as he waited for Danny to tell his idea.

The sparrow landed again about twenty feet away from the boys. She hopped a few feet and cocked her head to the side, peering at them with one beady eye. Then she hopped two more hops and cocked her head again. All at once she stabbed her beak into the dirt and pulled out a worm.

Danny sprang from the picnic table. Screaming and squawking like a crazy animal, arms flailing wildly, he descended upon the frightened bird. She took off in a flutter, dropping the worm as she fled.

Danny giggled as he bent over to retrieve the worm.

Holding the mangled specimen between his thumb and forefinger, he displayed it. "That, my fine friend," he proclaimed, "is my idea. It's the better way!"

Matt looked at Danny and then at the mangled worm. He burst out laughing, fell from the bench to the ground, and continued to laugh! It felt so good that he just let it come, until the tears were rolling down his cheeks. He laughed so hard that he thought his sides would burst wide open.

Danny flipped the damaged worm into the bucket. "That one counts for a half!" he said.

Matt stretched out on his back and looked up at Danny. "You are crazy. Do you know that?" he asked, trying to sound serious. "And that worm is damaged. We can't use it and we can't get worms from the birds either, birdbrain!"

"I know, I know," Danny said sheepishly. "It was just a thought!"

Matt picked himself up and slapped Danny on the back. "Keep thinking, Danny-boy! Keep thinking!"

seven

Gravel crunched under the tires as Aunt Marleen pulled the car into the parking lot of the ranger station. Matt hardly waited for the car to stop before he flung the door wide and leaped out.

"Come on, Aunt Mars," he called. "We have to go this way to find Patches's herd!"

Aunt Marleen shut the car door and followed.

"Slow down, Matt. I'm not as young as I used to be!"

Matt was so excited about showing Patches to Aunt Marleen that he had trouble slowing down.

Aunt Marleen didn't have a bicycle, so they had driven over the bridge to Assateague. July was usually suffocatingly hot, but today was warm and breezy, perfect for walking.

Aunt Marleen stopped to pull a can of bug spray from her sack.

"Come over here and let me spray some on you, too," she said. "There are a half a dozen mosquitoes clinging to the back of your legs."

Matt bent to brush the pesky insects away, then stood still while his aunt coated him with the spray. His legs and arms and even his face were already peppered with puffy red insect bites. But that was the way all Chincoteaguers looked. At least, Matt thought, I *look* like I fit in.

They walked down the trail in companionable silence. Aunt Marleen hummed a tune under her breath, stopping every so often to pick a daisy or cornflower and stick it in her hair.

The humming made Matt think about last summer, when he had walked down this same trail with his dad. Dad had whistled a little tune as they walked, sort of like Aunt Marleen was doing now. Matt could almost picture him. Almost, but not quite.

Matt looked out over the creek and into the marshes. He could see three Sika deer grazing way out. He remembered his dad showing him how to adjust the camera to get a clear picture from far away. More memories flooded him as he walked silently beside his aunt. He remembered crabbing in the bay with Dad and then seeing the ponies for the first time.

"You're awfully quiet, Matt. You were so excited in the car. What happened? Do you have something on your mind you'd like to talk about?"

Matt looked up quickly. "No. I was just thinking about the ponies" he lied. "There's the pony trail up ahead."

They entered the trees. A familiar odor was in the air. Matt smiled. He had learned to recognize the smell of the ponies. He turned toward the breeze. Stepping off the path, he pushed his way through the undergrowth. He knew there was a large meadow just ahead. The ponies often grazed there during the day. There was also a small pond of fresh water nearby for them to drink from.

"We aren't going to get lost, are we?" Aunt Marleen asked.

"No. I've been here before," Matt answered, excitement rising in his voice. "They're just ahead. I can smell them."

Aunt Marleen sniffed the air, but said she couldn't smell a thing.

Pushing aside a large branch of pine, Matt gestured toward the meadow. "There they are!" he exclaimed. "But I don't see the yellow pinto . . . or Patches!"

He scanned the field, searching the cord grass and weedy marsh shrubs, but Patches and his mother were nowhere in sight.

A sinking feeling came over Matt. Something was not right. He didn't know what it was or why he suddenly felt so afraid. His stomach turned anxiously. He was glad Aunt Marleen had come along.

"Something is wrong," he said softly. "Patches and the mare *never* leave the herd." He could feel a lump beginning to form in his throat, and he realized with horror that he was about to cry.

"They have to be here somewhere," Aunt Marleen reassured him, "and we're going to find them."

Matt wiped his eyes on his arm and willed himself not to cry. "We have to," he half-whispered.

"We won't leave the island until we do," Aunt Marleen said firmly. "Let's try this path."

This time it was she who led, pushing the way through the thorny bushes, holding back the branches for Matt. They followed a well-traveled pony trail away from the meadow and the rest of the herd. It wound its way through the wet bottomland, crossing several tidal creeks. Then the land rose sharply and the path led the way out of the marshes and through another meadow. They crossed a blacktop bicycle trail.

Matt followed his aunt half-heartedly. His drive and determination had been left back with the herd.

"Is that your colt?"

Matt jumped at the sound of Aunt Marleen's voice. Then he saw them, standing just off the trail. The colt was beside his momma.

His head hung down until his nose almost touched the ground.

Again the feeling washed over Matt. Something was definitely wrong! He approached them cautiously.

"Be careful," Aunt Marleen said, following close behind.

Matt stretched out his hand. The colt raised his head until his nose touched Matt's hand. Patches looked into Matt's eyes. Matt could tell the colt was in pain. He ran his hand down the colt's neck and over the shoulder.

The mare shifted her weight nervously then flattened her ears. Matt heeded the warning by stepping back, giving her time to adjust. His eyes finished the inspection his hands had begun, running down the length of the body and then the legs.

Patches swung his body sideways, away from his mother. Now Matt saw the problem. An aluminum can clung to his front hoof, crushed and bent to fit.

Aunt Marleen gasped when she saw. Blood oozed from the bottom of Patches's leg where the sharp, torn edge of the can had cut him. "Can we help him?" she asked.

Matt didn't answer. He moved forward, softly murmuring as he approached. "Easy boy, easy there. You're going to be all right. We're going to fix things. Easy, Momma. Easy girl. We're here to help."

The mare's ears came up as the soothing words came in a continuous stream. Matt didn't dare stop. It didn't really matter what he said. He knew it was the tone that mattered.

Matt ran his hand down the colt's leg. It had begun to swell just below the knee. He wondered how long the can had been attached so tightly to the hoof.

Patches stood quite still as if he understood the soft stream of words. He lowered his head and watched Matt as he ran his warm hand down the leg, but he didn't flinch. He seemed to trust Matt.

Matt tugged on the leg, lifting the hoof upward until it came to rest on his bended knee. He pried at the can. It was wedged very tightly.

Aunt Marleen moved closer. The mare snorted and flattened her ears again.

"Step back, Aunt Mars," Matt said in his singsong voice, never changing tone. "They've seen me before, but they don't know you."

Aunt Marleen stepped back. The mare relaxed.

Matt seemed to work magic on the two wild creatures. He tugged on the can again and again and yet the two stood quietly. Little by little the can was loosening.

Suddenly, the colt pranced backward, wide-eyed as the can finally released his hoof. Matt moved back to stand beside his aunt.

With a toss of her head the mare nudged her son roughly, then whirled around and headed down the trail. Patches followed obediently, the blood from his reopened cut trickling down his leg as he trotted away.

Relief washed over Matt, and almost at the same time he felt betrayal. Even though he knew the mare's instincts pushed her to rejoin the herd, he felt as if *he* had just been rejected. His emotions swirled. He wanted to laugh because the colt was free, to cry with loneliness, to shout in anger.

Matt spun around suddenly and hurled the can through the air. It bounced off a pine tree with a hollow thud. He ran down the trail after the disappearing ponies.

"Go ahead and leave me," he yelled. "I don't care! I don't need you! You're just stupid animals . . . so stupid that you don't watch where you step, so stupid that you can't even help yourself!"

He took a deep breath and swiped at the tears that streamed down his cheeks. "You might as well run away from me! Everyone else does! Go ahead and leave me! Just git!"

Matt fell to his knees. His anger drained away and he was filled with sadness. Then Aunt Marleen was beside him, kneeling in the grass, stretching her arms around him like a warm blanket. He leaned into her shoulder and sobbed. He couldn't hold it in anymore and he was too tired to try. His glasses slid from his nose and she took them silently, holding him like that, without speaking for a long while, until his tears stopped.

"It's okay to cry, Matt," she told him. "Sometimes it's the best thing to do." Tilting his chin so she looked in his eyes, she continued. "But you must never, ever think your dad left because of you. No one caused your father's death. It just happened, and we're only humans so we don't have the power to understand why."

Matt lowered his head. "I guess I know that," he mumbled into her shoulder. "But I miss him so much . . . and I miss Mom, too!"

"I guess you do." Aunt Marleen rubbed Matt's back. "But you have to remember why your mom sent you here. She didn't want you to stay alone all summer while she was at work. She didn't think it would be good for you . . . especially in the city."

Matt nodded. Aunt Marleen continued. "Your mom has a lot of loose ends to tie up at home. She'll get them all straightened out, and then she'll be here for you!"

Matt pulled away and looked up at Aunt Marleen. Hearing her reassure him made Matt realize how much she cared . . . and how much his mom cared, too! Reaching up, he hugged Aunt Marleen tightly.

"We better head back," he said finally.

"You okay now?"

"Yeah. I'm okay. Do you think the colt will be all right?"

"I think he'll be as good as new by the end of

the week. These island ponies are a tough breed, you know!"

Matt nodded and smiled. "Thanks!" he said softly.

The smell of bug spray, pine needles, and ponies filled their nostrils as Matt and Aunt Marleen turned down the trail and headed for home. It was almost dinner time, and Uncle Bob would be wondering where they were.

Even though the day was almost over, Matt felt like it was just beginning.

eight

A thick brown worm stretched out in the circle of light that Matt's flashlight cast on the ground. Quickly, he reached for the worm, but his thumb and forefinger came together empty.

He had missed again. Darn! He needed all the worm money he could get now that he was going to try to buy Patches at Pony Penning. He and Danny had already made two more deliveries that week and

Mr. Pringle had given them a raise. Now they were getting a dollar-twenty-five for a dozen worms. Still, he only had eighty-six dollars saved!

"Man! I missed again! Either I'm getting slower or the worms are onto us. Hey Matt, do the worms seem faster to you?"

Matt glanced at Danny. He was hunched over with his light.

"Yeah! They're getting away from me, too!"

"Maybe we should wind it up for the night," Danny suggested, rubbing the small of his back forcefully.

"Not yet," Matt cried. "We gotta keep trying to get them. Don't give up yet. Another dozen each . . . how about it?"

Even in the blackness that surrounded them Matt could see Danny's shadowed face as he straightened up and rubbed his cheek in mock disbelief.

"Am I hearing you right, or are the worms talking? Matt, are *you* saying you don't want to quit yet? Weren't you the one who said we were spending too much time worming?"

Matt smiled in the darkness. It was time to tell Danny about the colt. It seemed kind of silly keeping it a secret now. Before it had been important to have Patches all for his own. But now things were better. . . . It was time to tell his buddy.

"Okay. Just another dozen," Matt said again. "Then we'll go in and have a root-beer float and I'll tell you why I've changed my mind . . . why I need this worm money so much now."

Danny grinned in the dark and shook his head. Then he bent back over with the flashlight. His hand darted out and he drew a wriggling worm from the grassy lighted spot. "Okay. But this better be good," he challenged, as he flipped the worm into his can.

Danny poured two glasses of root beer while Matt scooped vanilla ice cream into each glass. It fizzled and foamed. Matt stirred his glass thoughtfully. Danny plopped himself into a kitchen chair and looked at his friend expectantly.

"I kept my part of the deal," he said. "One dozen more worms. Now it's your turn. What do you need the money for?"

Matt drew in his breath. "To buy a colt at Pony Penning," he told Danny.

Danny looked at his friend as though he were seeing a man from space. "What do you want with a colt? When you go home to the city you won't have a place to keep a pony! And even if you did have a place, what's the hurry? You could save for another whole year and get one next Pony Penning!"

Matt leaned against the yellow countertop. "I don't need a place to keep him. I read a story in the paper about a lady who bought a colt last year, then had it sent back to the island to live out its life, free forever. I can give him back to the island if I want to!"

"Now I really don't get it! Why would you do that?" Danny rubbed his face. He thought about what Matt had said. "Wait a minute," he piped up. "You said 'him'! Is there a particular colt you want to save?"

A smile slowly spread over Matt's face as he thought about Patches. "Wait a minute . . ." he called. Then he dashed upstairs to get his photos, Danny following behind him. He'd show Danny Patches so he could see for himself.

A moment later he spread the pictures out on his bed. "Isn't he a beauty?"

Danny studied the photos. Then he turned to Matt with a hurt expression. "Yeah! So how long have you been watching him?"

Matt hadn't counted on Danny feeling left out. "Since before I really knew you," he explained. "I guess I should have told you about him a long time ago, but I didn't really know you in the beginning. And then, it was kind of neat having him all to myself."

Danny shuffled through the pictures quietly. "I thought we were friends."

"We are! You're about the best friend I ever had . . . and I should have told you. I'm sorry."

Matt sat down beside Danny. They were silent for awhile, then Matt spoke. "I need that colt," he said softly.

Danny stacked the pictures, a look of determination filling his face. "Then we'll get him," he said.

Reaching into his pocket, he pulled out two crumpled dollar bills. "Add this to your savings. It's not much 'cause I'm not too good at saving, but from now till Pony Penning I'll pitch all my worm money in, too. Maybe we can save enough! I'll help you! It will be our goal."

Matt wanted to hug Danny. He wanted to cry, too, but he blinked it back. He hadn't realized what a good friend Danny was.

"Did I tell you I saw him being born?"

Danny shook his head. "Nope."

"It was my first day on the island and it was incredible! Look at these."

Matt pulled the photos of that day from the bottom of the pile. A skinny, wet, and wobbly Patches peered out at them. The colt had changed so much over the months.

Matt heard Danny's words, kneaded them, and mulled over them in his mind. The colt had been "his" for so long. It was hard to believe the word "ours" could sound so good.

nine

The bedsprings squeaked. Matt rolled over, wrestling with his sheets, trying to push away the sweaty feeling they made against his skin. He was hot and clammy, but as soon as he kicked the sheet off a mosquito began buzzing persistently in his ear, sending chills down his back. He pulled the sheet over his head, fanning it up and down to create a breeze.

It was no use. He couldn't sleep. So Matt's thoughts wandered as he stared upward at the eerie gray light filtering through the sheet.

Only two days until Pony Penning. It was hard to believe he'd been on the island for two months! Matt whispered another prayer that Patches would escape. He had visited the holding pen just yesterday. So far, so good. Patches and the mare had not been captured. But he knew the men would be out again, searching for stragglers.

Matt could make out the gray form of his dresser. He could almost picture the envelope of money, stashed in the top drawer under his socks. Danny had helped him with it. They had worked hard, digging bloodworms by day and picking up night crawlers at night. Now the bulging envelope held almost two hundred dollars! After Matt took the last cans of worms to Mr. Pringle in the morning, there would be over two hundred dollars. Matt knew the cheapest colt at last year's auction sold for one hundred and fifty dollars, but the most expensive one had gone for over a thousand dollars!

Matt cleared his head, turned his pillow over, and punched it down. The bottom side was cooler. A slight breeze rustled the curtains and whispered across him softly. Thunder rumbled. Matt curled his legs under him and dozed off to sleep. He dreamed of rain falling on Patches.

"Matt." The voice was a quiet and distant hum. "Matt." It grew louder.

Someone touched his arm and the bed sank lower beside him. Matt's eyes fluttered open, but he still wasn't sure he was really awake. In fact, he had to be dreaming, because he saw his mom.

"Mom!" Matt sprang up in his bed like a pogo stick as soon as he realized he wasn't dreaming. When her arms folded around him in a huge hug, he knew for certain she was really there!

"When did you get here?" he asked. Rubbing the last remnant of sleep from his eyes, Matt saw it was morning.

"Late last night."

"You should have woke me."

"I just did!"

"Last night I mean. You should have woke me as soon as you got here. I didn't even know you were coming!"

"I couldn't miss Pony Penning, now could I? I hear it's a really important one this year?"

Matt looked at her eyebrows arched in a question. She winked at him. "Well, isn't it?"

"Yeah! If Patches gets caught I'm going to buy him! But Aunt Mars already told you that, didn't she?"

"Yes, she did, but it didn't surprise me. When I got those pictures you sent me of the colt I figured he was a special one."

"Maybe we can go see him today," Matt ventured. "That is . . . if we can find him. I haven't seen him all week. I think the herd is in hiding. It's like they know what's about to happen."

"Well, they probably do. It happens every year, like clockwork."

"Isn't it kind of cruel, Mom? I mean they round them up and make them swim the channel. Then they separate the babies from their mothers. They whinny and cry for each other, but they never get to see each other again."

Mom looked like she was collecting her thoughts. Then she took his hand.

"It does seem kind of cruel, doesn't it?" she asked. Matt nodded and she continued.

"But it's really an act of great kindness. If the firemen didn't round up the ponies each year and sell the young ones, the island would get so overpopulated . . . there would be so many ponies . . . that they would starve and die a long, cruel, suffering death. The salty marsh grass over there is low in nutrition. The island can't support all of them."

Matt nodded. "But why do they make them swim?"

"There're too many to bring over by boat, but they do bring the oldest and weakest ponies and the tiniest foals over on a barge. They swim the ponies at the lowest possible tide, too."

"I guess the ponies are used to water, anyway," Matt said. "One day I saw a whole herd of them right out in the surf, cooling off!"

"That's right!" Mom laughed. "Now get up, sleepyhead. I'm taking everyone out to breakfast today!"

Matt grinned at the door as it closed behind her, then he jumped out of bed to get ready.

Breakfast was long and leisurely and Matt thought the food was about the best he'd ever tasted. But even better was the announcement Mom made.

"Aunt Marleen and Uncle Bob have found us a house to rent on the island," she said with a grin.

Matt dropped his fork in disbelief. "We're going to live here? For good?"

"That's right, Matt," Uncle Bob said. "Your mom has found herself a job as the bookkeeper at Sturgeon's Seafood House on the mainland. Looks like you're here to stay!"

* * *

After breakfast Aunt Marleen went to work with Uncle Bob and Matt took his mom to Assateague Island. They rode on bicycles around the "Wildlife Loop," just like they had the summer before, only this time Dad was not with them. Matt thought about Dad. He could picture him pedaling away, taunting Matt to catch up, until Matt took off after him. This time it didn't hurt to think about it. In fact, it felt good to remember.

"Let's check the holding pen first," Matt said to his mom. "Just in case they caught him." They pedaled in silence after that, Matt fervently hoping his words were not true. Their bikes bumped up and over a rise in the path as they turned onto the short dirt trail that led to the holding pen.

The pen was packed with ponies of every shape, size, and color. One old black stallion, tall and lanky, stood over his mares in the far corner. Matt and his mom propped their bikes against the fence next to the stallion's herd.

"Look at his teeth," Mom whispered as though the old stallion might hear her.

The stallion's upper teeth jutted out at an awful angle, barely meeting his lower ones. From a distance he had looked so beautiful. Up close, with those teeth, he looked pathetic.

Matt pulled his camera up from around his neck and snapped a picture. "Mr. Pringle told me the sand on the marsh grass grinds down the ponies' teeth," he told his mom, "but I never saw anything like that before."

They moved down the railing and away from the stallion, scanning the herds. Matt's eyes skipped over the bays, chestnuts, whites and blacks, and settled on the pintos. He held his breath each time he found a yellow pinto or a patchy brown colt.

"I never realized there were this many pomes," Matt said. "Most of them I don't even remember seeing."

They worked their way around the fence slowly. Matt kept one hand resting on his camera, stopping to snap a picture here and there. Just when he was about to let out a sigh of relief, he spotted them.

The yellow mare was in the center of the pen. Patches dozed beside her, his nose shoved up against her flank as they both stood switching away the bugs. Then Matt saw the brown stallion and he realized the whole herd had been captured.

Matt's mother saw him stop and stare. She saw his smile fade and his hands drop to the board fence, and she followed his gaze.

"Is that Patches and his momma?"

Matt nodded. Mom laid an arm across his shoulder. "Maybe you'll have enough," she said.

"Maybe . . ." he whispered numbly.

ten

Matt brushed a mosquito from his face. The sun was glaring, reflecting the metallic water into his eyes. He wished Danny were here. Of all the times to get the chicken pox, now was the worst. Matt thought chicken pox was supposed to be for little kids, not for nine-year-olds! Well, there was nothing he could do about it, so Matt sat alone, hunched on the black rocks, waiting for the ponies to swim.

While he waited, Matt turned up the smaller rocks piled on the jetty. He scraped snails from the bottoms of the glossy stones and pitched them to the fish. Every now and then a tiny crab would scurry from under a rock and wave one large claw over his head like a boxer protecting his face.

Matt looked out over the water again. He tried to imagine what it would be like for Patches. Would the men be whooping and hollering like a thousand gulls when they descended upon the ponies? Would Patches leap away from the noise and follow his mother into the water? Would he be afraid?

He skipped a stone across the water forcefully. Then another and another, until he was hurling them, watching the bubbles rise and the circles widen around them as they sank.

The sun rose high. Earlier, when he had arrived at the park, the crowd was thin, but now there were people everywhere. Matt moved farther out on the rock.

Matt thought about his mom. By now she would have read his hastily scribbled note, "Leaving early. Meet me at the swim. Love, Matt." She was probably here now, looking for him. Matt turned to look for her, but a roar rose from the crowd. He shaded his eyes and scanned the water.

There they were! His heart pounded as he watched the ponies plunge into the channel, a blur of colors. He stood on the rocks and watched them swim closer. Boats of every size and shape formed a passage for them to swim through. Matt whispered a prayer for Patches. He worried about all those thrashing hooves.

Now he saw the ponies clearly, their heads lifted high in the churning foam, their noses pointed toward the shore. The crowd parted as the first ones scrambled ashore.

It was weird how quiet everyone got as the ponies filed from the water, wet and tired but seemingly unaffected by the crowds. They wandered ashore, lipping up mouthfuls of grass as they walked.

"The grass is always greener on the other side of the bay!" someone joked. A few people giggled, then everyone began to talk again.

The yellow-spotted mare was in the middle of them. Patches plodded along beside her, dripping wet and confused. He looked so different, all wet and thin. Matt lifted his camera and snapped a picture. Patches stopped to stare.

"Hello, boy," Matt whispered, but his voice blew away with the breeze and the colt turned to follow his momma.

Matt followed the ponies and the crowd through the park and down the road to Main Street. He felt like he was part of a parade. People lined the streets on foot and in lawn chairs. They shouted and cheered as the ponies went by.

At the carnival grounds the ponies were driven into a huge pen. The mares settled down to graze, the foals to nurse. High-pitched squeals rang out as the stallions nipped at their mares, bunching them up, separating them from the other herds. The brown stallion pushed his herd to the far corner of the pen.

As he watched the colt, fear grew in Matt until it formed a hard lump in his stomach. The auction was only a day away. Two hundred dollars had seemed like so much. But was it enough?

Matt pressed his face against the chain-link fence, watching until it left diamond-shaped impressions in his cheek.

eleven

E ven though it was only eight o'clock, the morning sun already sizzled down. It rose like a hot red ball behind the crowd, burning their backs as they waited to watch the auction. Matt fanned himself with a piece of paper. He removed his glasses, wiped the sweat from his face, then replaced them again. His mom noticed his fidgeting and placed a hand on his knee.

They had arrived a full hour before, setting up their lawn chairs in the front of the area sectioned off with blue ribbons. It was a good thing they had, for now the crowd was as thick as mosquitoes and the chairs were at least six rows deep.

As two men separated the last of the foals from the mares, the auctioneer joked with the crowd. Matt didn't listen, for each time the husky nicker of a foal rang out, he pictured Patches weaving by the fence, calling out for his momma.

"Now folks," the auctioneer rang out. "We're gonna give you a look at a real special Chincoteague pony."

A man walked into the ring leading a tall, brown and white pinto mare. Every hair on her body glistened and she almost shimmered as she walked. Beside her was a pretty little pinto filly. The mare tossed her head as if to say, "Don't we look good!"

"This here's Windy, her filly Wind Storm, and their owner Michael Pryor. Windy's a granddaughter of the famous Misty of Chincoteague," the auctioneer continued, "and she's here to show you folks what a difference good care can make. You buy one of these ponies here today, take it home and clean it up and feed it right, and it will look this good!"

Matt felt a shiver run down his spine. Windy and Wind Storm were absolutely gorgeous! Windy's mane fell in a cascade of silvery-white strands as she marched across the ring proudly. Could Patches look that good, Matt wondered.

As Windy and Wind Storm left the ring, the auctioneer grinned. "Here we go!" he called, as the first foal was wrestled onto the platform. Matt wiped his clammy hands on his jeans and watched. The little palomino pinto stood on its hind legs, surging forward as it came down. The two men holding her sweated, groaned, and fought to hold her still.

"Hate to tell you folks this," the auctioneer said, "but these colts ain't been taught to lead yet! You'll have your work cut out for you!"

Matt smiled at the frisky little foal.

"What we got here is a pretty little filly. You can tell by her coloring that she's probably out of the original Misty herd. Now what do I hear?

Who'll start the bidding?"

A man two rows back raised his hand. "A hundred dollars," he shouted.

Matt groaned. "They're starting them at a hundred," he told his mom. "They're gonna go high."

Mom patted his knee and smiled. "You don't know that yet," she reassured him firmly.

"A hundred and fifty," the auctioneer droned. "I got a hundred-fifty. Who'll give me more?"

The little boy next to Matt tugged on his daddy's arm. "Come on, Daddy," he pleaded. "She's a Misty pony!" The father smiled and held his hand up.

"I got two hundred!" The auctioneer slapped his thigh excitedly. Then he stopped talking and it was quiet a moment. "Now folks," he said softly, "I gotta tell you. This here is one of the best in the bunch. The first one out and the last one to go are always the best ponies to buy."

The crowd laughed and the bidding began again. A moment later the filly was sold for two hundred and seventy-five dollars to the man with the kid next to

Matt. The kid threw his cowboy hat high in the air and jumped up and down. "Is she really mine?" he squealed. "Is she, Daddy? Is she?"

The auctioneer droned on, shouting numbers, recognizing bids, trying to get the top dollar. One by one the foals were led out to the platform. The crowd smelled like oil and bug spray, hot dogs and crab cakes. They were smells the foals had never smelled before. They danced and reared and kicked their protests. But in the end they all had to go. Some of them balked and had to be pushed out. Others fought like warriors. But Patches did neither. When the men led him out he stood quietly, his head hanging with dejection.

Matt wanted to cry. It reminded him of the day Patches had been injured by the can. The same look was in the foal's eyes.

"This here's a pinto colt with some super markings," the auctioneer began. "He's a little on the young side so he'll probably need some foal feed to start him off. But he's gonna be a looker! Who'll start the bidding?"

"Fifty dollars!" someone yelled and Matt sighed in relief. It was starting low.

"I got fifty! How 'bout a hundred?" the auctioneer asked.

Matt raised his hand. "Seventy-five!" he called in a shaky voice. Mom's hand gripped his knee.

"Okay, son. Seventy-five! Do I hear that hundred?"

"A hundred!"

Matt's stomach churned. "One-fifty!" he shouted.

"One-seventy-five!"

Matt turned to see who was bidding and saw a woman with her hand up. "Two hundred," she shouted. A man two rows behind her followed with a two-twenty-five bid.

Matt felt his body go numb. It had all happened so quickly and he didn't even have a chance.

"I wish I could help," Mom said grimly. "But I just don't have it."

"Three hundred!" the auctioneer shouted. "Yes,

sir! We got a nice-looking colt here. He'll make a super riding horse. He's got size, folks! He's got size!"

Oh, shut up, Matt thought. Just shut up. He stood and the lawn chair crumpled under him.

"You all right?" Mom asked.

Matt pretended he didn't hear. He turned and wove his way through the blurry cloud of figures, stumbling through the tall pine trees and onto the carnival grounds. He was aware of the money in his pocket, a wad of hope gone sour. Maybe he'd spend it on the rides. Maybe he'd spend it all.

He stopped at a bench in front of the bandstand. Sinking onto it, he rested his head in his hands. Patches had not only made his summer special, he'd taken the sadness away. How could he lose him? He kicked dust up with the toe of his sneaker. Tears formed behind his eyes. He was too weak to hold them back. Too weak to care.

A hand came down on his shoulder and Matt looked up. Aunt Marleen, Uncle Bob, and Mom stood solemnly beside him.

"Tough luck, kiddo." Uncle Bob murmured, then he lifted his hand from Matt's shoulder. "Come with us?" he asked. "We have to show you something."

Matt noticed his mom was crying but also smiling through her tears. "There's something you have to see," she said.

He didn't want to move, but Matt didn't have the energy to argue either, so he followed them back through the carnival grounds and the pine trees, back to the holding pens.

"Look at that," Uncle Bob said slowly.

Matt looked up, and his breath caught in his throat. It was Patches! He stood alone with that horrible red sale tag tied around his neck.

Matt knelt next to the fence. Pulling his camera up, he snapped a final picture of his Patches. To his surprise the colt's head came up in recognition. Then he rumbled a low greeting and walked over to the fence, pressing his nose through the wire at Matt.

"Looks like that's where he belongs," Uncle Bob

said and Matt felt even worse because he had let the colt down.

Uncle Bob continued. "He's yours now," he said softly.

Matt fingered the colt's whiskery nose through the wire. Then Uncle Bob's words registered and his heart did a sideways jump. "Mine?" he leaped up to ask.

"When the bidding got high, I stepped in,"

Uncle Bob explained. "We bought him for you, Matt. He belongs with you."

Tears streamed down Matt's face again, but this time they were tears of joy. Patches was his. Matt wanted to hug and kiss them all. He wanted to scream and shout. But first he did what he wanted to do the most. He knelt down and pressed his face closer to the colt. The colt nuzzled him gently.

"I love you, Patches." Matt said it softly, savoring the way it felt to say it out loud, how good it felt not to be sad anymore.